ISABELL

SHARON WANKHEDE

Made with ❤ on the Notion Press Platform
www.notionpress.com

"To all the women out there, you are strong."

Contents

Preface

Isabell In Red, is a story that shows a young strong woman in the form of a serial killer. I have written this book to send a message. This book expresses courage of women. I can relate to the concepts of the story. At the end, I hope the readers enjoy the story.

Acknowledgements

I would like to express my gratitude to my father Mr. Sanjeev Wankhede, my mother Mrs. Wilma Wankhede and my elder brother Mr. Sagar F. Wankhede for being my pillar of strength. Their care, support and love has helped me through the toughest times, especially while writing this book.

CHAPTER ONE

Can you relate what it's like to have a dark secret you can't afford anyone to have the privilege to know even a word of it? Well, after almost 9 years today, I will be interviewed by a journalist, Ms. Katherine Jones. I am nervous revealing secretive events from my past, but I firmly believe I'll have the courage to do so.

After few hours I step out of my house for the interview, my heart is pounding faster, I start breathing heavier. "I certainly want to do this and I can do this. I can do it; I can do it." I keep ranting these affirmations to myself as I walk a few blocks away. I'm not nervous for myself, I am worried will they ever find her or is she gone forever? Giving secrets to the media, I'm afraid whether she'll come back to me or will I never get to see her again.

"Mr. Joseph," somebody calls out my name from behind.

I turn behind, she introduces herself to me "Good morning Mr. Joseph, I am Katherine Jones. It's a pleasure to meet you."

"Good morning Ms. Katherine. I hope I'm not late." I greeted back.

"Not at all, you are just on time. Thank you for agreeing for this interview." She spoke.

Ms. Katherine takes out a notepad and a pen from her bag. She pens down my name along with the time. She looks up to me and asks "are you nervous?"

"I slightly am, I answer."

"It's okay, it'll be fine." She comforts me.

I look down, I take a deep breath and I ask her to begin.

Mr. Joseph, you know the reason behind this interview, I want to know the beginning of it and the end, how were you in custody for the murders and then released after few months. Would you like to reveal it to us and specially about her?

I tell her it's going to take a lot of time to hear every little detail. "Do you have the time for it?" I asked.

I think we've all waited to know the truth, even if it is going to take days to know the full story, I am fully committed to this. There were many other reporters who wanted to know your story, but you never really let them interview you. Why is that so? Suddenly after 8 years you have agreed to tell us, I want to know what's behind the curtain. So yes, Mr. Joseph I would immensely spend my time knowing the truth.

Ms. Katherine seemed to be a genuine, kind-hearted and a lovely person. I have read a lot of about her in the Daily times. She has written books on the vices and quarrels of politics and has interviewed many politicians. I know for a fact that she strives for the truth and justice. Katherine is phenomenal in her work. She has achieved greatness in her work for the poor and the rich. I have agreed to come only for her interview because she is a trust worthy person through ways I've read about her and her work.

CHAPTER TWO

I stay quiet for a minute, I did not utter a word from my mouth, but I knew I had and wanted to. So, I begin telling Ms. Katherine.

It was 9 years ago, I was waiting outside the restaurant at 8.30 PM for my date, I'm looking around and I almost believed my girlfriend has forgotten about our date night. I'm about to take off, I stepped down. My phone slips from my hand. I rush to pick it up and it starts to rain. Its not a rainy season, why the hell is it raining right now? I raise my gaze towards the sky, the thunder! The lightning! The Breeze! The sound and the light have all my attention. I love the way the breeze hits my whole body, giving me goosebumps. It's cold. And wow, Goa looks amazing when it rains. Just as I am admiring the beauty of Goa, I hear footsteps at my right, I see a woman heading towards me, - she's covered with a warm peach dress, a pendant necklace, wearing an old watch and doesn't really care about the world. Her black heels, may be 3-4 inches, stole my attention from the weather. Maybe she does like a little attention.

She is walking towards me all wet, whilst covering her head with her hand bag. She has long, slightly brownish black hair. She stood beside me outside the restaurant under a small tilted shelter. I can't get my eyes off her, she is beautiful, her eyes, and her pinkish lips. Gosh! Doesn't seem to be a woman who would start a first conversation, but she looks towards me and with her soft, seducing voice she asks,

"Gentleman, do you have a phone?"

Yes, I answered.

"Could you lend me your phone for a minute to make a call, please? My phone's battery is dead."

Of Course, I gave her my phone and I still can't get my eyes off her. She had the most attractive eyes I've ever seen.

She dialed a number, the ending was 7896 "Hello, Mr. Borges. It's raining heavily, I can't come home tonight. Could we meet tomorrow? I hope that's okay, please don't get angry, it's not my fault, it started raining heavily all of a sudden. I'm in Panjim. I have to run some errands. I hope you understand.

The Speaker on the call (Mr. Borges yells with his heavy croaky voice): I will not tolerate this nonsense anymore, you had to be home by sunset, where are you? Get back home you............!

I eavesdropped the conversation with a heavy heart. She was victimized, her heart had sunk and she looked every bit vulnerable. She cut the call, disgruntled.

She returned my phone and hesitantly thanked me with a strained smile. I wanted to be kinder to her after hearing the conversation so I asked her if he needs any more help,

Instead, she asked me "Could you please accompany me in the Taxi?" seemed frightened.

I was numb, I didn't know what to say, I wasn't really sure if I wanted to, wasn't even a familiar face in the neighborhood, why is she asking me to go along with her? But I really couldn't say no, I had to.

"Yes sure." I answered.

CHAPTER THREE

We share a taxi now and it's pouring. We are heading towards Chapora. It'very awkward here, been an hour, no words spoken, yet it seems so noisy, never knew silence could be so loud. I wish to get out of the taxi but I shouldn't. I want to make sure I drop her home safely. I realized I haven't even known her name,

"I'm Joseph." I introduced myself in a belief that she would do the same, but no. She just stared at me disgracefully. I felt embarrassed and no longer wanted to share the taxi. I was about to ask the taxi driver to drop me ahead.

She said "Isabell. My name is Isabell." And smiled. I looked at her and smiled back.

Her perfume odor was tempting. Exquisitely aromatic and exotic.

She opened up a bottle of juice from her handbag asked me if I wanted to have some, I refused and thanked her. She couldn't hear 'No' for an answer so she pleaded me to take a sip.

Should I or should I not? Murmuring to myself, I was thirsty anyways.

I took the bottle from her hand and I sipped. This juice is the best juice I've ever had. It is sweet, has small pieces of strawberries in it and red in color. So fresh! what is it? The moment I opened my mouth to take another sip, the driver applied a harsh break, and I spilled all the juice on my white shirt. I felt ashamed and angry. On the other hand, Isabell laughed whole heartedly.

And again, this time I stared at her for a long time, she has a beauty spot slightly below her lip, mischievous dimples and mysterious eyes. I couldn't wait any longer to talk more to her.

I asked her "what is it that makes you so attractive?"

She looked into my eyes for a few seconds and asked. "Why do you find me so attractive?"

Your beauty spot below your lip. I answered.

She got goosebumps; I saw it. She was quiet and she looked outside the window.

And oh! My white shirt got red and messy.

We reached her house after a few minutes, her bungalow was light brown in colour, with huge glass windows, two floors with a balcony and a heavenly garden with a fountain.

"Take care Isabell, have a safe night." I said goodbye.

"Why don't you come inside? Please come, the least I can do is help you with another shirt." She requested.

I didn't want to go in, it would be really tempting, but I chose to agree her offer with an excuse. I convinced myself that I'm feeling extremely cold, my shirt is wet which makes me feel colder and I need an another one. But am I really feeling cold?

I uncertainly said yes. And she took me along with her inside the house.

CHAPTER FOUR

The house had 17 steps to climb, it was exhausting. But as soon as I entered the house my tiredness died out. I was astonished, speechless, stunned or whatever adjectives used to describe a house that's imaginarily breathtaking. It was less about the decor and more about the paintings hung all over the house. They were magnificent. I wanted to have a closer look at them, I happened to turn back and ask Isabell if I could have a closer glance at the paintings. She was out of sight. Where did she go?

"Isabell, Isabelllll......" I shouted.

"I am here, at the closet". She replied from upstairs.

"Could I have a look at the paintings around?" I yelled.

"Yes sure," she responded.

Each wall was decorated with 8-9 paintings, it got me standing on a stool to see each one of them. These paintings were elegant, comprising of a different emotion attached to each and every one of them. There were messages, feelings, story, morals and a lot more. From a scenery, that showed a girl playing with her friends below the sun to a woman's face expressing horror, pain, wrath yet bold and strong, there were all kinds of paintings -forests, mountains, waterfalls, even a painting of her own house. Western to eastern she had everything hung up on her wall. From Surrealism to Korean. All impressive. A painting that was unique or would rather say scary drew my attention from the others, a man's hand was painted red and black. It looked deadly and massacred, what was the painting revealing? I slogged to relate it with the other paintings but still accomplished no clue.

She came down with a blue shirt. I told her these paintings were incredible.

“Are these all your art?” I asked.

She nodded her head proudly and answered “yes.”

It was unbelievable, she was unbelievable. I was speechless.

“Here, you can wear this, I hope it levels your expectations!” Isabell handed me the shirt.

“Indeed, a great choice.” I spoke.

I went in a room to change my shirt, and I see books displayed all over the room. Now it gets exciting for me, I really want to know this woman more, who exactly is she? Is she an artist? Is she a writer? A bookseller? I suddenly see her peeping into the room as I am changing, she comes inside the room and she says that I have a strong muscular body, I was a bit shy and I couldn’t really say anything, I just said thank you! Well, I am more sexually drawn to her now. I see a photograph of a famous politician, on the study table and there were different maps marked with a red marker, I inquisitively asked, are you heading somewhere? And is this, Alfred Gonsalves? You’re related to a famous politician? Isabell looks at the photograph with revenge, hatred, and anger in her eyes. I tried to drag the topic a bit more but couldn’t.

“Would you like some coffee?” She politely asked.

“Yes, I think I would love that.” I answered.

As Isabell headed downstairs, I was had a doubt that something mysterious is going on. This house, the paintings, the books and the maps were all a bit of a mystery. I wouldn’t leave spying on her now.

But as I was heading downstairs along with her, I noticed a room that had a huge lock on it. It wasn’t a lock usually used just to lock a room; it was a huge metallic lock. I particularly found this sight scary as all the other room have no locks.

I ask Isabell “Is that your room?”

She turns behind me, she smiles at me with a hidden motive behind that room and says absolutely nothing.

Isabell asks me for a cup of coffee and as I wanted to discover more about this beautiful mysterious woman, I surely wanted to have a chit chat with her. She heads towards to the kitchen and I start exploring her house.

CHAPTER FIVE

After few minutes, I go to the kitchen and I see her making coffee. Oh Gosh! She's still beautiful. Am I falling for her? I doubt, I need to be careful. I ask her, "how do you always look so beautiful?" and again she answers me with a question- 'why do you always find me beautiful?' I blushed.

We were seated at her balcony having coffee, she gazed at me, at my lips and I know this because I was staring at her too. I wanted to hold her tight and kiss her. As I was thinking of it, she left her seat and requested me to kiss her, I was almost about to drop dead, did she really just ask me to kiss her? I tried not to give a weird expression on my face, but no, my mouth was just left open, my nose widened, my eyes got bigger and I felt this strange urge deep into my chest to kiss her.

She laughed, obviously my expression deserved a laughter after all. I stared at her continuously. She walked towards the table and sat right in front of me. I panicked. It's not that I haven't kissed anyone before, I have. I am always the one who initiates the first move.

She saw me shivering, she asked me "May I have the permission to kiss you Mr. Joseph? I said yes, but why do you have to ask? I am the guy; I need to ask for your consent.

She replied, "well, I don't think so. I believe consent is very important for all people regardless of their gender. Whether a man or a woman, bodies are being equally touched and shared by both, then why not an equal consent?

I couldn't agree more, I caught her hand and slowly brushed my fingers through her hair. In no time I surrounded her waist with my arms and we kissed. It was slow, relaxed and peaceful. I loved every ounce of the moment. We stared into each other's eyes for a long time, I thought I'll better pack up and leave, but I lost to my heart.

See, my heart and my mind don't reach to a final table of agreement, we fight, but that day, it forced me to break all the barriers, it quarreled for what it needed and I had to bow.

She took me to her room, I undressed her, her body looked heavenly, but seemed like she didn't want to have a sexual intercourse, she felt uncomfortable. I understood her body language. There was something bothering her.

"Isabell, I can sense that you don't want us to be sexually intimate partners, but can I hug you and sleep?"

"I feel that's okay. Yes, you can." Isabell answered.

We slept the entire night, cuddling each other.

The next morning as soon as I woke up, I thought I would have the lovely sight of her sleeping besides me and I would prepare a delightful breakfast for her. But nothing turned out the way I planned. I woke up with a horrific sight. I see Isabell walking through the corridors with a knife, she was wearing a sweatsuit that had blood stains and her hand looked like as if it was dipped into a bucket of blood. It dripped on the entire corridor as she walked. I was frightened. what did she do? Did she murder someone? Am I going to get murdered next? These thoughts were racing in my mind. I didn't really understand what to do at that moment.

CHAPTER SIX

I went back to my room, I was shivering, I thought I should get out of the balcony, but as I opened the door, I heard

"Mr. Joseph, a very good morning to you!" Isabell greeted.

"Uh-ah! Good, good morning to you too Isabell." I hesitantly greeted back. Her hands looked washed but the blood stains were still visible on her sweatshirt and she had a painting along with her.

"I went for a morning walk at the hill. I captured the sunrise on my camera. It was a breathtaking view. I have painted it just now. Would you like to see it?"

She shows me the painting, I went blank for a while, it was magnificent. I questioned myself, how can somebody be so talented and beautiful ever do something wrong? So, I took up the courage to ask her, "Isabell, I see that you have blood stains on your sweatshirt and few minutes back I saw your hands masked with blood, would you like to explain me a reason for it?"

Isabell answers "oh yes, actually that's not blood, its red paint, I was cleaning the paint that fell on the floor while I was keeping the pack of paints back into the shelf. What a misery early morning! I need to buy new colors."

I wasn't completely convinced with her answer. I wanted to smell that paint. But I didn't. Was that really paint? Is she lying? If she is, then why? What has she done? I had to know who she really is but I couldn't wait any longer, I had to get back for work.

"Isabell, I hope I'm not being rude, but I have to get back to work, I need to go, I will return in two days. Last night was the most beautiful night I've ever had my whole life."

"I will be waiting for you, come back soon. Goodbye Mr. Joseph."

I left. Oh! My Girlfriend, Monica. I completely forgot to enquire why she couldn't make it yesterday. I sat in a cab and called her.

Joseph: "Monica, are you fine?" what happened yesterday?

Monica: "Hey, listen... listen, I had a meeting with a client yesterday, I tried calling you but your phone was engaged and later, switched off. I am very sorry about last night, what did you do last night?

Joseph: "I went home and did my laundry. "

Monica: "Can we meet today?

Joseph: "Actually, I need to run some errands. We could catch up tomorrow.

I lied. What else should I tell her? That I was with a woman. It would just mess up things.

I reached the psychiatry clinic; I was very curious about Isabell. I google up the name, Isabell Gladlin. I find absolutely nothing. No social media accounts, no evidence of her existence at all. Who is she? Is it even her true name? I must go to the Government office in Chapora and seek for information.

CHAPTER SEVEN

"Hello sir, Good morning, my name is Joseph Baldwin. I'm a psychiatrist working at the Psychiatry Hospital at Panjim." I greet an elderly grumpy government employee.

"Hello Mr. Baldwin, how can I help you?" he answers with his heavy voice.

"I am attending a client who seems to be in danger and I need to get some additional information about her. Could you please help me out here?"

I give him Isabell's address. He goes inside the locker and gets all the documents that match the address. There were 200 documents.

He says "You can check these few documents."

Few! Really? That's few for him! Of course, after all he is a government employee. I'll take ages to finish all of them and when I even do, I'll surely end up dead. The documents were ancient, dusty, rotten, damp, brittle and yellow. How am I even supposed to go through all of this, and oh! There's fungus formed on one of them. I roll up my sleeves and I start digging. I don't even feel like touching it. I turn pages of one document and they just come off the file. I can read nothing that's typed on these pages. Its 4.00 in the evening and I find nothing related to her in almost 107 documents.

The grumpy employee yells "Aren't you done yet?"

"uuhhhh! No sir, my body is unable to turn into a machine"

"What! its just 200 documents." He yelled.

Again- Just, really? Just 200?

"Let me help you." He said.

He starts digging along with me, he goes through 3 documents, he seems so engrossed into the pages and doesn't lift up his head at all. Suddenly he shouts with excitement, "here it is, Isabell Gladlin's Birth certificate." And I yell "what! 107 documents and nothing, you go through 3 and you find the treasure. He smiles like a child when he hands over the birth certificate to me. I guess a simple achievement can bloom a person, it's just the way the person perceives the achievement. For an elderly man like him, finding an important document is a classic achievement. He is not as grumpy as I thought he was. I lovingly thanked him and I left with the birth certificate.

I headed towards the hospital in which Isabell was born. Saram hospital, 7km away from the government office. I enter the hospital and ask the nurse for a reference to this birth certificate of Isabell Gladlin.

She says, "it's against our rules to reveal any information about our patients." I didn't try to convince her. As I was leaving, I heard a man from the back say "Did you just say Isabell Gladlin?"

I turn back and answer "Yes Mr. how do you know her?"

He starts walking towards me. He was a young man and seemed to have a good heart.

CHAPTER EIGHT

He smiled at me and spoke. “We were neighbors in Velim when we were 7 years old. We were best friends. Her parents passed away and she disappeared. I tried to find her but I couldn’t get any records of any sort. Why are you here with her birth certificate? Do you know where she is?”

“Yes, I met her yesterday for the first time.” I answer.

“Wait what! You met her yesterday for the first time and today you are holding her birth certificate, what’s the scene?” He doubtfully questions me.

“Listen, uhh! I’m Joseph Baldwin, What’s your name?” I hesitantly introduced myself.

“I’m Clifford.”

“Clifford, could you tell me more about Isabell, I’m her therapist. I need to know more about her.” I asked.

“A confident personality with a generous heart, she was the heart and soul of our colony. I remember everything about her, she was playful, joyful and beautiful. Our neighbors called her the most talkative girl in the colony. She would dance to almost every song, sing and paint anytime of the day. Isabell also knew how to play different musical instruments like the guitar, violin, piano and the flute. She cooked all types of foods. Everything was going fine, but one day, she came home and cried bitterly, we tried asking her the reason, but she didn’t utter a word. She refused going to school for some days, the colony turned quiet because she was quiet. After few hours, her house blew up in a fire incident. The neighbors filed a complaint to the police, but as far as I remember the police refused to file the case. And after two days her parents were found dead in one of the lakes in the North. The police closed this case as a suicide case and didn't look much into it. Isabell went missing after this and she never returned back." Clifford explains.

"Were your parents and neighbors convinced that it was a suicide?" I Ask.

"No, I mean, none of us were ready to believe that it was a suicide, they were well to do. He answers.

"Isabell still paints, she has paintings all over her house, but the one you are talking about many years ago is not the same, she isn't joyous anymore, I guess. There's a lot of secrets I'm yet to find out and I will, thanks to you for sharing this. This history will help me a lot." I thanked him.

"I wish to meet her one day. Could you give me her phone number?" he requested.

"Uh! I actually don't have her number. My office files may have her number." I lied.

"Okay, never mind. See you. Bye." He left.

I feel sorry about Isabell's parents and for Isabell. I like Isabell, I do. But I need to know more, where did she disappear all these years? Who is she now? Was it really a suicide? Why didn't the police look into this matter deeply? I'm confused, I want answers. I just met her yesterday and I've known so much yet less. Wait a minute, she made a call yesterday from my phone, I start checking the call logs on my phone and the number has been deleted. Why did she delete it?

Well, I have one more lead on my investigation. 'Mr. Borges'

CHAPTER NINE

It's a new day today. I'm in my house sipping coffee. The doorbell rings and its Monica.

"Hey Joe, I got you a doughnut." She speaks.

"Come on in Monica" she gets in and I shut the door. I hug her tight.

I tell her that there is something she needs to know, "Monica, listen, I'm glad you came today. I have something important to confess."

"Yeah, feel free to tell me anything Joe, what is it about?" Monica asks.

"We have been together for almost 6 years, it has been so wonderful and I am so grateful that you gave me a chance in your life, this journey has been incredible. But honestly, I have fallen out of love since many months, I don't know the reason. The relationship that we have feels different, I feel different. I think that you need to know the fact. It is difficult, but it is the truth. We should part ways Monica. We need to individually focus on ourselves."

She is quiet, I ask her "Monica, why aren't you saying anything?"

I'm listening to you Joe, tell me more about how you feel?

"Since few months I have been feeling caught up, I am not blaming you for it, it is not your fault, it is just that I haven't been myself lately and I feel that right now I only need to sort out certain things I am confused about."

"How are you feeling right now Monica?" I ask with a guilt.

"I am glad you spoke the truth and you built up the courage to tell me this. Joe, if you are really up for this decision then I am not going to stop you or say anything, is there anything else that you would like to talk about?"

"Monica, how are you so cool on this? I mean does it not make you feel angry or sad?"

"Joe, I am feeling sad. But, right now, I need to keep my feelings aside and consider how you have been feeling. I have never seen you look so vulnerable before. So, I need to make sure that I understand you. If you need to talk more about anything, let me know. You know you are not lonely."

"I am still so grateful to have you in my life. Thank you for being so understanding."

"I should leave for work Joe. If you need any help, just give me a call."

"Bye, take care Monica. Text me once you reach the hospital."

Monica handled the situation very maturely. Monica and me were best friends since school. We both knew that if ever our relationship ends, our friendship would never sink. It was a deal and we strived hard to grip on that.

CHAPTER TEN

As soon as Monica left for work, I continued my research on Isabell Gladlin. I noted down every little detail on my book. And I carried on for my work.

I enter my clinic; I start taking sessions. I love my job; I've always wanted to be a psychiatrist. I really enjoy having meaningful conversations with people. While having sessions, I realize a lot about myself, about how different people perceive the world differently. Unresolved matters, unique desires, uncontrollable situations, every little aspect of what people do in these situations has an underlying reason to it. It can be a simple soft reason or a major deep one and diving to the depth of it is what really drives me in this profession. At the end, things eventually settle down, everything gets better no matter what the situation is. All we need to do is continue to have patience and have faith in ourselves till it gets better. Every human being is similar yet unique. We have all desires but it differs, we all have feelings, but the intensity matters. We all want to love and want to be loved. Love cures the universe.

I come from a small village; all I knew was how to survive. We had neither clean water or food. My parents hardly earned 50 rupees a day. I strived hard to become worthy. I worked every small job I got. I didn't deny any opportunity, from cleaning people's houses to cleaning garbage on the road. I saved every penny I earned. When I observed boys of my age, they were bathing in luxuries. But the only thing I needed was to fill my stomach which was difficult to do. We lived in a small house which had just one room. My parents worked hard as well to provide me education and food. We didn't receive clean water from the tap. So, we used to extract water from the trees. It was a tedious job. I felt that pain of hunger. I wasn't the best student at a government school in my village. I was a decent one, I would complete my homework regularly and I tried to look clean. I had no friends in particular. There was just one classmate who was kind to me, his name was Karan.

Karan helped me once when my father was ill. He saw me working hard for money to buy medicines for my father. He himself went to buy medicines from the store without even letting me know and gave it to me the next day in school. I haven't forgotten those who have helped me in my toughest times. I always have respected them and in return would want to offer them. I firmly believe that human beings just need a small amount of money to survive. We need food water and shelter. Nothing else matters. A decent job that can provide us decent amount of money to fulfill their needs. But the greatest hurdle in this path is that we want more and more and this never stops.

It's in our nature to want more than we have. This leads to competition, jealousy, anger and hatred. We ourselves have created a world in which we find it difficult to live in. I wish we could go back to the time where we could just hunt, fill our stomach and live with peace and love.

This period is a race where we can't see the end line. A race of expectations. When we don't see the end line we keep running, along the way we sometimes realize we don't even know where we are going. We are clueless as we keep running, there's disappointment because we just don't know where to stop. If we knew when and where to stop, more than half of the world's illness would never be to such a great number.

CHAPTER ELEVEN

As I go back home late evening, I realize I just have very little information about Isabell.

Days pass by, neither I get a call from Monica nor Isabell.

I decide to go to meet Isabell. But firstly, I had to check on Monica.

As soon as I reach home, I already see her in the house.

"Hey, I was about to call you." I spoke.

"Joe, I had an extra key of your apartment. I thought of returning it back to you." Monica sadly said.

"No. I think you should keep it with you. Don't return it back to me." I try to convince her.

"Okay."

"Would you like to have dinner with me? I ask.

"Sure, I would love to" she answers.

I wash up and we start cooking together. I enjoy cooking with Monica. She is fun and brightens up the place. But today she seems to be different. I ask her about her day but she doesn't seem to respond the way she used to.

I ask her "Are you disturbed because of our breakup?

She doesn't say anything to me but looks at me with tearful eyes and slowly she starts crying. I make her sit. I wipe her tears.

I apologize – I am sorry for hurting you. Is there anything I can do to make you feel better? I'm really sorry Monica.

I couldn't see Monica crying. She is after all my best friend.

Monica speaks- I understand, but I am feeling bad. I know you are hiding something from me. I can sense that. What is it, Joe? The reason you gave for our breakup wasn't the genuine reason. There is more to it and I need to know.

Monica was right. I broke up with her because I developed feelings for Isabell. This was wrong at my part. I couldn't keep dating Monica. But I don't know whether I should tell her about Isabell. No, I won't.

I hug Monica and I tell her that yes there is more to it, but you aren't the reason for it. You are lovely, it's not your fault, you did everything right in the relationship and I appreciate everything about you.

"I am not yet ready to tell you, I need to understand things by myself first. I will surely tell you when its time."

Monica cries on my shoulder and says "I know I will feel better after sometime. I just need to let it all out." I kiss her on her forehead. We start eating dinner, I had to take care of Monica. I ask Monica to spend the night here.

I felt guilty that night. I know I can be better than this. I am a good person. I shouldn't hurt a woman; this was all what I was taught by my mum as I was growing up.

CHAPTER TWELVE

I carry on with my investigation next morning. I head towards Isabell's house. I certainly feel that I need to search every corner of the house.

I ring the doorbell, the house care taker opens the door for me.

"Good morning, Sophia"

"A very good morning, sir" – we greet each other

"Where is Isabell?" I ask

"She has gone out for a walk. She will be back soon." Sophia answers

"Hmm, morning walk I see, she likes keeping herself fit." I playfully said.

"Sir, would you like to have a cup of coffee?" Sophia asks.

"Oh no no! I would just like to wait for Isabell. Thankyou."

Sophia heads towards the veranda. It is the perfect time for me to search the house. I climb upstairs, I enter Isabell's room. The maps that were displayed all over were scratched and removed. I search for the key of the cupboard in the drawer and I open the cupboard. All I see is different shades of red dresses. I put my hand a little deeper in the cupboard. I find Alfred Gonsalves' photos. There were photos of him clicked secretly. A photo of him travelling in his car, meetings, appointments, his house, his room, his garden, and his guards. As I was looking at the photos carefully, I find a blueprint of his house and there were markings done on it with arrows towards his room.

My curiosity increases. What is the relation between a famous politician and Isabell?

I carefully keep the photos in its place along with the blueprint. I close the cupboard; now I go towards the mysterious room which is always closed. How do I open the door? It has a huge lock.

Where can I find the key? As soon as I start searching for the key of this room, I hear Isabell's voice from behind.

"Mr. Joseph, what are you doing here?" Isabell nervously asks.

"I was actually...hmm...... searching for my ring. I guess it fell down the other day." I lied

"A ring? Interesting. But the time I met you, I do not recall any of your fingers wearing a ring." Isabell doubtfully answers.

"Right....it was in my pocket." I hesitantly lied.

"Are you lying to me?" She asked.

"Not at all." I answer

"I can sense that you are lying to me and you were not searching a ring. Are you searching the key to this room?" She angrily questioned me.

I couldn't lie anymore to her. I respond back by saying yes.

"Why do you want to go inside this room?" Isabell heatedly asks.

"I want to know the reason why this room is always locked. I need to have a look inside." I answer

"You must respect my privacy and space. I do not allow anybody inside this room and I can't let you inside as well, Joseph." She strongly said.

I had no option. I did not want to argue more with her. I had to be close to her to know her truth. I told her I will not try to find out anything about that room.

CHAPTER THIRTEEN

We go out for breakfast; I try to cheer Isabell up.

"What would you like to eat Isabell?" I ask.

"I am in a mood for pancakes. What about you?" she hungrily answered.

"I will eat pancakes with you too."

While we were eating the pancakes, I asked Isabell about her parents.

"Where do your parents live?

"They passed away when I was a kid." She sadly answered.

"I am very sorry, what happened?" I asked her.

"An accident." This is my mother's watch. I know its old. But I love it, it reminds me of her and everything else. She replied.

I decide to ask nothing more to her. She seemed sad. I had to stop asking her questions about her parents.

Although she has secrets, but somewhere I did love her. I gave her a hug.

Do you need anything else Isabell?

"No" she answers.

From what I understood is that Isabell is a strong woman, physically and mentally. She has been alone for a long time. No friends and no family. She choses to not need anyone. She is self-sufficient and self-reliable. Isabell "You remember you had made a call from my phone the other day, who was that?"

"Mr. Borges" – she answers

"Who is Mr. Borges?" I ask.

"I worked for him for a very long time." She responds.

"Now you don't?"

"No"

"Why so"

"He is dead." She calmly replied.

"When and how." I shockingly ask

"Few days back, his neighbor found his hands and legs in a lake next to their house." Isabell answered.

I was shocked to hear about Mr.Borges. I surf through the internet about him. It turns out that he owned a multinational company and his co-partner was Alfred Gonsalves. Now that he is dead, the company is owned by Alfred Gonsalves alone. Did Alfred Gonsalves murder him for the company? I drop Isabell back to her place and I head towards my office. I turn on the radio of my car to distract my mind. I hear that Alfred Gonsalves is in custody, for murdering Mr. Borges for the company. This allegation has been put by Mr. Borges' brother. Mr. Borges was beaten up with a rod all over. His head was smashed. His face wasn't recognizable. The murderer chopped his ears and his genitals. He was harshly banged on the wall. His body was chopped into pieces. Before he was chopped to death, boiling water was poured all over his body. The police found his ears and genitals at Alfred Gonsalves' house. The rest of his body parts were still missing. Everybody in Goa was shocked. All day and night, the media repeatedly kept discussing about this incident.

CHAPTER FOURTEEN

I know for a fact that all this is somewhere linked to Isabell. I had to figure out a way to know more.

As I enter my office, I already see a client sitting inside. The client is Maria Gonsalves. Alfred Gonsalves' mother. Well, Maria Gonsalves was one of my clients few years ago.

"Hi Maria, after a long time." I greet her.

"Joseph, how are you?" she greets me back

"I'm okay. I'm seeing you after almost 3 years. How are things with you?" I enquire.

"I am so not in a good state." She gloomily answers.

"Tell me about it, Maria."

"My son Alfred, he is in custody. He is a suspect in Borges' murder case." She speaks.

"Yes, I heard about it. It must be terrible for you." I respond.

"I can't see my son behind the bars. Although we have our differences since many years." Maria cries.

"I completely understand. How do you feel about this?" I ask.

"I am frightened, lost..... I don't know how to get my son out of this situation. I don't think he can escape this time." She responds.

"Could you elaborate more, please?" I ask

"She is back. I know she is back and she will not leave anyone alive. She will take her revenge and maybe she should. After all what happened to her, what these guys did to her and her family is unforgivable." She terrifyingly answers.

"Maria, when you say 'She' whom are you referring to?" I enquire.

Maria doesn't answer my question she becomes silent for a while.

"Alfred and his friends did wrong to her and her family years ago. I just can't say her name. I have no courage to. I knew the truth but to save my son I agreed to his terms. I shouldn't have but I did. This is eating me alive. I feel terrible and guilty. I feel that I don't deserve to be living so lavishly. I have failed as a person but I tried hard to be a good mother to him, which got me nowhere closer to my son. After knowing the truth, I neither could look at my son nor give him any love, although I did love him a lot." She spoke.

"Maria, I know you have been trying hard to be a good mother to Alfred and because of this struggle you decided to save your son. I am not saying this was the right decision, but you have been feeling guilty since many years and as you said, it is eating you from inside. Maybe we could think that feeling guilty about the decision you made makes you a good person. Can we?" I try to comfort her.

"I guess so. But this doesn't change the fact that I gave in for something evil." She responds.

"Well, you could start by explaining me what 'evil' are we talking about?" I curiously ask.

"I wish I could tell you more about this Joseph, but I can't. I have assured my son that I won't tell his secret to any soul. I am just so confused. He deserves to get punished for what he has done but as a mother I am feeling sheer sadness." She answers.

"I understand. I wont force you to tell me details you don't want to. But if you ever feel like opening up, you are always welcome here. But remember that you are a good person and you are working hard for yourself." I respond.

"I am going to take off, thank you so much Joseph."

"Take care, Maria."

CHAPTER FIFTEEN

I try to interpret Maria's unspoken words to me. What has Alfred really done? And who is 'SHE'.

As I keep sorting out the tangles, it gets even more puzzling.

I decide to visit Mr. Borges' brother. I go to his office few miles away.

"Hi, Sherwin. Good afternoon" I greeted.

"I am Joseph Baldwin; I am a psychiatrist."

"How can I help you Joseph" Sherwin replied.

"I know this isn't my place to enquire any personal information, but I need to know about Mr. Borges. If you could...." I requested.

Stop stop! He yelled.

Are you a reporter? If you are please leave right now.

"No, I am not from the media, I think I know who has murdered Mr. Borges and that is why I am here to discuss it with you. Please let me.

"Okay, so tell me who has murdered my brother." He questioned.

Before I give you a hint, I want to know about Mr. Borges.

And why would I do that? Sherwin angrily asked.

Joseph: I know you are in a very crucial phase of your life right now; nothing must be making sense to you. You will get pass through this. You need answers as well as I do. I understand if you don't want to speak anything but if you do, it will surely help us both Sherwin.

Sherwin: Borges was a good brother, he was kind, careful and had clear intentions. I wonder if he could ever harm somebody. He respected every human being whether rich or poor. Why would anyone even murder him?

Joseph: I know it's hard to imagine something as unanticipated as this when you got the news.

Sherwin: The police informed me. They brought the body home. The forensic reports disclosed that he was burnt on few areas of his body, his hand specially. The killer banged his head on a hard surface and strangled him to death and then cut his body into small pieces. It was a planned murder. But why would someone murder my brother? What has he done? I know for sure he wouldn't hurt a soul. He was a good man. After few hours the police found a DNA match on a weapon in my brother's pocket. It matched clearly with Alfred.

Joseph: If Alfred murdered Mr. Borges, why would he leave a knife in his pocket?

Sherwin: That is what I am confused about. Was he so careless or was he so stupid?

Joseph: Why would Alfred what to murder Mr. Borges?

Sherwin: My brother and Alfred were co-partners of the firm. They earned a huge profit together. Alfred wanted to buy another company under the firm, Borges was against it because the company that Alfred wanted to purchase deals illegal stuff. He had a fight with Alfred and convinced him not to buy the company. Alfred did not adhere, he went ahead. That's the reason my brother wanted to be the owner of the company by himself so that he could take decisions, or I should say right decisions by himself. I had no idea this fight would turn into a murder one day. The police knows about the illegal trading. I had to tell them.

Joseph: This is a huge matter. But I don't think Alfred has killed your brother Sherwin. I think there's more to the story we are yet to find out.

Sherwin: I hope so.

Joseph; I know it is difficult, but you are a strong person Sherwin. Hang in there. Take this as a challenge and stay strong and courageous as you are.

Sherwin: Yeah. I will try.

Joseph: Take care

CHAPTER SIXTEEN

The next day, I hear a news of another murder. Two bodies were found at the same lake where Mr. Borges body was found. The victim's name was Stevan Sirino and Cristian Las. This time, the killer drilled Stevan's body through his abdominal, leaving a huge whole, chopped his tongue and shot his eyes. Cristian's body was found in two separate parts with each being burnt. Such a frightening terrible death.

I decide to meet Isabell at her place. I know Isabell has answers to my questions.

I talk to her about this murder case, she doesn't seem shocked.

"I heard about it, Joseph. I wonder what the killer wants to convey through the murder." That's all she said.

I ask her directly "Do you have anything to do with these murders Isabell?

"What do you think?" She asks.

"I really don't know. But I don't want to blind myself. But at the same time, I feel that you would never harm a soul." I emotionally reply.

"Do you trust me?" Isabell questions.

"I am finding it hard to. I feel that you know something about these murders." I answer.

She doesn't utter a word, leaving me clueless.

I go close to her I hold her waist gently, I stare deep into her eyes and I request her "if you are in any problem or even if there's information you know about these murders, please talk to me about it, Isabell, I feel exhausted searching for answers."

"Why are you so eager to know about these murders?" She angrily questions me.

"I have this strange feeling that these incidents are largely linked to us, but I can't seem to figure it out. Help me, Isabell."

"It's okay if you don't figure it all out yet, eventually you will." She replies.

This time as I stared into her eyes, I could feel a sense of darkness that longed for light.

I wait for few days, no more murder cases reported yet, Alfred Gonsalves is still in custody and the media splashing its different views and assumptions about the murders have no end.

'Alfred Gonsalves plans these murders with his associates'

'Alfred Gonsalves is a murderer, hang him to death.'

'He is a drug dealer and a corrupted politician'

Everybody blamed him for these murders.

Once the media portrays something, it is believed to be the truth. The cases are being investigated by the FBI. Beautiful Goa turned into a nightmare.

CHAPTER SEVENTEEN

The next morning the police reports that Alfred Gonsalves goes missing. They couldn't track him. His mother was questioned, yet no information. It was claimed that he fled away from the police.

I get a call from Alfred's mother.

"Joseph, you have to save Alfred"

"Maria, he has escaped from the police, what is going on?"

"I will explain everything but for now please save him, he hasn't escaped. He has been kidnapped." Maria was frightened.

"I don't understand, by whom?" I ask.

"It's her. I will send you an address, you will find him with there. I can't trust anyone else with this matter, please do not inform the police, I beg you."

"Wait, why not inform the police?" I doubtfully ask.

"Please trust me, Joseph. I want my son home. Get him safely home, she will kill him."

I head towards the given address by Maria as fast as I can. I head down quietly towards a basement. It was a dark, gloomy scary basement. It had blood stains all over the ground. I hear screams of a man. "Please let me go, somebody help me." As I move closer, I see Alfred Gonsalves tied up on a chair with his mouth slightly taped. He was brutally tortured and was scared to death.

I start running towards him to save him but as I do, I hear a woman's voice from a corner of the basement. I hide behind a huge barrel.

The voice sounds familiar. The woman is wearing a red dress, with her hair left open. She was burning a huge metallic iron piece.

"Alfred, your vices have created a huge impact around the world."

As she turns around and says "you have to be punished." I was shocked, it was Monica.

I watch her silently. She takes the hot iron piece and burns Alfred's hands.

Alfred breathes heavily and screams with pain.

For a moment I blanked out, I realized that Monica is responsible for all these murders. She also seemed to disappear suddenly, neither did she come to work nor did she respond to my texts.

Suddenly everything seemed to be crystal clear but yet, blurry. Now that I know Monica is responsible for these murders, but I fail to understand why does she have to kill all these people.

As Monica burns Alfred's hands, she makes a sound. I wonder what was she saying. She turns behind and looks at the barrel. I hide myself from her.

After a few seconds, I sneak again. Monica constantly stares at the barrel. And this time she notices me hiding. I almost started running to escape, she nodes her head left to right with fear, and moves her lips as if she was trying to give me a signal, I was pulled behind with a black sac covering my face tightly. I couldn't see anything. The sac contained chloroform. I tried really hard to escape the grip of the person pulling me, but I couldn't. I was getting drowsier and I fell unconscious on the ground.

CHAPTER EIGHTEEN

Aaaahhh! I wake up with soreness in my entire body. I couldn't feel my legs. I find myself tied up on the chair the same way as Alfred was tied up in the same dark shady basement. I don't understand how can Monica do this? But as I think deeper, I realize that Monica was standing in front of me and I was pulled from behind. It was somebody else who made me unconscious. But why would Monica not save me?

I feel thirsty. I start shouting out for help. Suddenly, I hear a soft weak voice from behind, "Joseph, Joseph help" I turn behind. I see Monica tied up on the chair far behind me.

"Monica? What is going on." I yell.

"I am sorry." Monica apologizes.

"Sorry? You killed all those people brutally"

"It wasn't me joseph."

"Then who was it? I saw you burning Alfred's hands. How can you even do such a thing?"

"It was..."

The moment Monica was going to tell the person's name, I hear a melody of Harmonica musical instrument. The tune was filled with agony, injury combined with rage and vengeance along with footsteps from the dark side of the room walking slowly towards the light. It was a woman. As the woman neared the light, I saw her face.

I was astonished, it was Isabell

"Hi, Joseph." Isabell greets.

"I knew it." I angrily yell.

"I know. But you didn't inform the police. Even though, you could have."

"Why Isabell?"

"You will have all your answers Joseph. Some Patience."

"Enough of these secrets and these lies. It is exhausting. I have had a lot of patience with you. I have shared all of my secrets with you, and you don't share anything. Am I nothing for you? Why have you tied us? Are you going to kill us as well? You might as well kill me, Isabell." I was frustrated.

Isabell stares into my eyes silently, doesn't utter a word.

"This annoying silence, again. I can't stand it anymore. Tell me what the hell is going on." I yelled at Isabell.

"I would never hurt you and Monica." Isabell answered.

Isabell brings water and hands it over to us and walks away into the dark silently.

After a few minutes, I hear her footsteps again. I also hear another voice; she drags Alfred on the ground while walking towards us.

"It is time for you both to witness the death of a demon." She said.

"Isabell what are you going to do? Why are you killing all of these people? Do not commit another murder. Please" I begged her.

"Didn't Monica tell you the story behind all these murders? The reason why I have killed all these monsters?"

"I haven't, don't have the guts to." Monica answered

"Fair enough. I will explain each and every detail to you."

She leaves Alfred on the ground. She starts sharpening a Falx. As it starts to clatter, Isabell speaks

CHAPTER NINETEEN

"Few years ago, when I was 12 years old, I was a happy middle-class girl, lived with my lovely parents and my younger sister. I spent my days beautifully, got up, made my bed and I dressed for school. My mum used to make breakfast for us. After having breakfast, my dad and me left home for work and school. He would drop me off to school every day in the morning, we happily lived in a colony. You might be knowing this very well Joseph? Don't you? Didn't Clifford tell you this?"

"How do you know I met Clifford?" I shockingly questioned.

"I know you were investigating; I observed every step of yours each day. You also found my birth certificate, didn't you?" she replied.

"I did."

"And what did you accomplish by finding it?" Isabell questioned me.

Isabell was wearing a red dress. I had no idea why would she have a preference of only one color. She takes a chair and sits in front of Alfred with the sharpened falx under the light, while he seems half dead on the ground.

I loved my parents more than anything in this entire world and I would do anything for them. Anything.

One day, I was returning home from school. I had a lovely day at school. Got praised from my classmates and teachers for the completion of my homework. I felt proud. I wanted to rush home and tell my mum about it. As I was walking home, I noticed a huge truck driving towards the forest. Until that moment I never saw a soul walk towards the forest. Not even the villagers. This was a huge truck which I have never seen before. The streets were empty and I was the only person along with the huge truck. I was curious to know where the truck was going. The truck stopped few meters away. I walked towards it, one man gets down from the truck with gloves, he unlocks the door behind the truck, two men get down from the back door of the truck. I hide myself behind a tree as quick as I could. I thought they were thieves. But why would thieves come into the forest?

They carried heavy sacs from the truck and went deep inside the forest. I followed them quietly. Those 3 men reached a location where there were two more men standing. They dug the ground and they sneakily kept the sacs in that space. As they were keeping it, I heard them talking

"Kilograms?

48

While a man was lifting the sac, he dropped it on the ground, as it was very heavy.

"Careful, its drugs." Man 1 – Stevan shouted.

"Don't say it loudly you fool. Sir has told us to keep this low. Don't you understand? Man (2) yelled.

"Sorry" – Stevan apologized.

I was shocked to see this happening in front of my eyes.

One of the men opened up a huge sac, he pulled out a hand from the sac and dragged the full body out of the sac. It was a girl's dead body. She was undressed. She might be around 18 years old. There were marks on her body as if she was forced. I could clearly understand that she was raped terribly by these men. I saw the injuries on her body.

I was panicking, I didn't know what to do at that moment. I started breathing heavily. My body was shivering. I had to gather courage and inform the police. The moment I took a step behind, I slipped on the rock. Those 5 men noticed me and one of them shouted "catch that girl."

I began to run as fast as I could. They all started chasing me. I was about to exit the forest. I see Alfred Gonsalves standing in front. He had just started his career as a politician, very powerful and almost had the entire government in his fist. I ran to him for help. I told him that I saw 5 men with a dead body and sacs of drugs in the forest. They are burying it. You must inform the police. Those 5 men reached near us, I told Alfred they are the ones, they are chasing me, help me. We must go and tell the police.

This guy, instead of helping me pushed me back into the forest. I yelled and cried for help, but there was nobody around. They dragged me to the forest near the sacs and tied my hands with a rope. While they were burying the sacs and the girl. I screamed for help and cried my eyes out. I was terrified. I wanted to go home to my mom and dad.

One of the men asked "What should we do of the girl?"

"What else can we do, finish her." Cristian said.

Alfred, didn't want me dead at that moment. He said "Before finishing her, let us finish her thoroughly first. What do y'all say?".

"Sir, I think we shouldn't it will simply create a missing case in the village. Missing case will lead to clues and someday finding those clues we will be caught." Stevan said

"We should let her go" Man 3 said.

"But what if she opens her mouth to the police?" Cristian asks.

Alfred drags me closer to him by holding one of my legs. He squeezes my mouth tightly with his hand, stares into my eyes with anger and blackmails me.

"If you open your sweet little mouth, I will sweetly come into your house and disrupt your entire life" (Isabell strongly stamps Alfred's face while talking)

He harshly pushes me back on the ground and pokes a needle on my finger till I bleed as he does this, he stared at me and laughed at my pain. I felt helpless and sacred.

They left me there and ran away. I cried and yelled for at least 3 hours. I couldn't move. I was shocked. I had to pick up myself and go back home.

I went home, I saw my mom and I wanted to explain her whatever happened in the forest, I wanted to express how frightened I am. But I had to zip my mouth.

Alfred wanted to rape and murder me. I felt powerless, he did touch me and I could do nothing to save myself.

CHAPTER TWENTY

My mom noticed that I wasn't okay. She asked me "What happened Bella? Did anything happen at school?"

"I am fine mom, just exhausted."

"Okay, go have your food"

While I was having lunch with my mom, I realized that I shouldn't keep quiet. I have to inform the police.

I got up from my chair and ran straight out to the police station. I left an anonymous tip about the girl who was raped and murdered and the drugs. I was scared to directly inform them, in this way Alfred and his men wouldn't know that it was me who informed the police.

I felt satisfied that I informed the police at the right time.

It took me an hour to reach home. The moment I reached home my entire life changed. I couldn't stand as I saw my mom's dead body in the kitchen. A bomb blast blew away my house and my mom.

Within a fraction of seconds, my dad was pushed down on the ground by Alfred's men and they took his right hand and chopped his fingers. My sister was shot. They picked up my parent's bodies and threw them at a lake. My sister's body was nowhere to be found.

As Isabell narrated, she took the sharpened falx and chopped Alfred's hands, she screamed loudly with all the pain she buried in her heart and the anger in her eyes.

Monica yelled; she couldn't see this anymore. She was scared but she knew that Isabell wouldn't harm us.

Isabell slowly drags Alfred to the sawing machine.

Then, they went near my mother's dead body and chopped each of her body parts front of my eyes.

Isabell places Alfred on the sawing machine, although Alfred wasn't dead, but he knew that this was it for him. He told Isabell "If you do this, it means you and I are the same."

Isabell yells at him loudly while turning on the sawing machine and pushed his head under it. "Alfred, your vices have created a huge impact around the world, I am nothing like you."

In a second Alfred was murdered and his blood was spilled all over on Isabell's body and everywhere else in the basement.

Isabell dropped down on the floor and cried the entire night holding her mother's watch close to her heart.

I couldn't do anything to help her or comfort her. I wish I could hug her.

I tell her "Isabell, it's over now."

She said, "no, it isn't. My revenge is still incomplete. The police."

They knew that Alfred was the one who committed such terrible crimes, they found the body and the drugs. They got it published on the papers and they were rewarded for their good work, but they didn't hold Alfred as the culprit, the police instead informed the media that my parents were the dealers. Alfred bribed the police to do so and the about the girl who was raped, no news was spread out.

Isabell, I know you've faced a lot, but can you forgive them? You have already murdered Alfred and his men.

I can't Joseph.

Why did you kill Mr. Borges?

To get information about Alfred, I had to work as an employee in his company. Since Mr. Borges was his copartner, he would often visit the company. One day, as I was heading home, I saw Mr. Borges physically abuse a young girl who worked in his company. The girl screamed and cried for help. I couldn't see this, I wanted to help but as I ran to his cabin the guards outside stopped me. I tried to file a complaint against him as well but no one took it into consideration. I spoke to the girl but she refused to speak up as he was blackmailing her. What he did was wrong and he had to pay for it. I don't feel guilty for killing him. He deserved a cruel death. He had to be punished for his doings.

CHAPTER TWENTY-ONE

"Why me Isabell?"

"Do you remember the first day I met you." She asks.

"Yes."

"It was all planned. Sophia delayed her session with Monica. Sophia had no personal interest to get therapy. She went for me, so that I get to meet you. Also, I never made any call from your phone." Isabell said.

"Why would you do this?" I question Isabell.

"I had to get you in my life because you had information about Alfred."

"I did not." I answer.

"Yes, you did, I stole your notes of your sessions with Maria Gonsalves. Who would know a person better than his own mother?

Although I worked in his company, but I couldn't get his personal information. One day I followed Maria. I saw her getting inside your office. What else would she speak about rather than her son's vices.

I judge every person I see. Just by having a glance, I know. You are a kind-hearted person, Joseph; you would never do anything wrong. I trust you." she explained.

"Whatever time we spent together, whatever we had between us, that comfort and care, was it all planned too?" I was heartbroken.

She stayed silent.

Why drag Monica in all this?

At some point in her life, she has also been touched in a wrong way or has been treated badly by a man. All women do experience this. I kidnapped her and I explained her everything. I filled her with rage. All I had to do was just remind her of her past.

She untied us and for two days we had no idea where she was. Monica and me, not even once thought of informing the police about the murders Isabell had committed. We didn't weren't on Isabell's side but we weren't against her as well. Alfred Gonsalves continued to be as a missing case. Days weren't normal, it took me time to accept for was done with Isabell's family and what Isabell did.

After a few days, I got a news about a police inspector of Goa, 'missing.'

Of course, it was Isabell who kidnapped him.

I went to the same basement where Alfred had to pay for his sins.

When I reached the basement, I saw the police inspector tied up with a chain to the wall same as a prisoner. He was beaten up terribly. His face was disfigured and was unconscious.

At the side I see Alfred's mother – Maria tied up on the chair with her mouth tapped.

"Isabell, why have you tied up Maria? What was her fault?"

"Her fault?" Isabell angrily questions me.

"She supported him for all the evil he has done."

"So? You will kill her as well?" I question her.

"I intend to"

"Isabell no, you can't. She hasn't harmed you. I will not let this happen." I tell her.

Isabell takes a gun and aims at Maria. I use my physical force to take the gun from her hand, but she pushes me away on the ground.

Maria screams – Help me, please. Help!

She pulls the trigger as she walks closer to Maria and aims at Maria's head.

I get up, I calmly talk to Isabell this time "Isabell, listen to me, give me the gun, I know you have a lot of anger and hatred to anyone or anything that is related to Alfred, but killing his mother is not a good way to take away your pain.

"Don't try to talk me out of this Joseph, she deserves this. She should have taken an initiative when her son was raping young innocent girls and then murdered them. She knew it and she did absolutely nothing. She supported her son every day. She knew what her son did to me and my family, she knew about the drugs as well. I hate this woman. She is the main cause for everything."

"Isabell, I know she shouldn't have kept quiet after knowing everything, but did she commit a crime, did she ever hurt you by intentionally in any way?"

"No, but" she said.

"She is innocent. Will you ever feel happy later when you realize that you've killed an innocent mother? Maria is my client Isabell, I know she wished her son would have some empathy towards others, but he did not. How much would she explain her son? It's not her fault that her son walked on a wrong path and committed evil doings. She tried her best, Isabell. Parents can try their best to teach their children to be courteous and mannerisms, but at the end it depends on us. Hand me the gun Isabell." I try to explain her.

Isabell slowly hands over the gun to me and cried bitterly while she hugs me.

Right after we hugged Isabell snatched the gun from my hand shoots the police officer leaving no bullets left.

We hear siren. Isabell forces me to leave. I refused to do so.

I grabbed the gun; I wiped her fingerprints and I tell her to run.

"Why Joseph?" She asked.

"You know why." I replied.

"I don't want you to be punished for my crimes. This is wrong." Isabell said.

"I won't be behind the bars for long. Do you love me, Isabell? I ask.

"Why do you ask?" She replies me back with a question.

We stared into each other's eyes.

We heard the police climbing down the basement.

"Go Isabell go. Run as fast as you can."

As the police arrives, I hold the gun.

They hold me in custody and take me to the police station. I am their new suspect for all the murders.

They questioned Maria,

She uttered only these few words to the police "Joseph is not responsible for these murders. He was being framed."

Those were her final words and till today neither did she speak a word nor did she ever step out of her house. She was traumatized.

After few months of torture and interrogation by the police I was left out. They had no concrete evidence that I had committed these murders. In fact, Isabell murdered so smoothly that she left no evidence of any sort behind.

When I was left out, I reached out to Monica. But Monica had already left the country.

I visited Isabell's house. It was burnt down.

After few days, I receive a letter. It was from her.

"Joseph, I owe you an apology. I am sorry. I had to leave. I am somewhere no one can ever find me. I am not a cruel person. I don't intend to be one. To what I did, is unforgivable, but I had to do this for my parents and for my peace of mind. All these years I was burning in hatred and anger. This wasn't the way to make things right. I hate men when they treat women unkindly. These murders were not the only murders I have done. I have murdered nearly 170 men till today. I have punished them the same way or even worse than I have done with Alfred and his men. The men I have witnessed or known to have eve teased, molested or raped women, I have killed them brutally. Including men, who have ill-treated and raped their wives as well. I wear a red dress when I murder them because I believe red signifies courage, boldness and power. I feel strong when I wear red. It gives me a sense of superiority over my fears. But as I kept exploring, I realized not all men are evil. My dad was the most amazing person in my life, he never harmed any women or anyone else. Then I met you, the way you treated me I found similarity the way my dad treated my mom. I know this is a wrong way to give a message to all the men in the world. I don't feel guilty for my doings. Instead, I feel proud. I feel that I have achieved victory. Men need to respect women and women need to respect men as well. But men who don't respect women, I punish them. I know you definitely are disappointed with me for not showing up. I can't face you ever again. Even if you try hard to find me, I never will be found, no matter even if the police get a hint about me, I won't be found. I hope you move on and start a family. You are a gentleman. I wish you luck. The answer to your last question -Yes, I do Joseph. -Isabell

Katherine: Did you start a family?

Joseph : I could never move on. I know she won't come back, but I still long for her.

Katherine: Do you still love her?

I smile and I say nothing.

I love Isabell, it has been almost nine years now, she never turned up. Its two days after the interview, I hear a knock on my door, I open my door and I see a box outside my door. I open the box and I am shocked; it was Isabell's red dress along with a man's finger.

9 798890 261151

Printed by Libri Plureos GmbH in Hamburg,
Germany